BETWEEN STARS AND STEEL FINGERS

A Spiritual Journey

Bebe Butler

Author's Tranquility Press
ATLANTA, GEORGIA

Copyright © 2024 by Bebe Butler

All rights reserved. No part of this publication may be reproduced, distributed or transmitted in any form or by any means, including photocopying, recording, or other electronic or mechanical methods, without the prior written permission of the publisher, except in the case of brief quotations embodied in critical reviews and certain other noncommercial uses permitted by copyright law. For permission requests, write to the publisher, addressed "Attention: Permissions Coordinator," at the address below.

Bebe Butler/Author's Tranquility Press
3900 N Commerce Dr. Suite 300 #1255
Atlanta, GA 30344, USA
www.authorstranquilitypress.com

Ordering Information:
Quantity sales. Special discounts are available on quantity purchases by corporations, associations, and others. For details, contact the "Special Sales Department" at the address above.

Between Stars and Steel Fingers: A Spiritual Journey / Bebe Butler
Hardback: 978-1-964810-65-2
Paperback: 978-1-964810-28-7
eBook: 978-1-964810-29-4

Contents

GREENLIGHT DARES 1

TWO SISTERS AND A SHORE 2

(cont) Two Sisters 3

GOD'S WISH 5

LAKEWATER OF STARS 7

(cont) LAKEWATER OF STARS 9

THE ODD STREAM 10

(cont) THE ODD STREAM 11

NEW SKIN 12

(cont) NEW SKIN 13

INDIAN DYES 14

(cont) INDIAN DYES 16

FREEDOM SONG 18

A SONG TO THE DIVINE 20

THE WARM ETERNITY 23

IF NOT TODAY 25

ZERO 27

UNARMED WHISPERS 29

LOSING NAME 32

HOME 34

CAUTION 36

THE QUEEN 37

WINDOWSILLS	39
WIND AND ROOTS	42
QUIET LIGHTNING	44
ONE INSOMNIAC DREAM	46
ON SOLID SKY	47
SUMMER MOON	48
ETERNITY	50
YOU ARE	51
(cont) YOU ARE	52
WIGGLER'S FARMER'S MARKET	53
(cont) WIGGLER'S FARMERS MARKET	55
CHILI SAUCE	58
COMMUNION	59
(cont) COMMUNION	60
MIRAGE	61
(cont) MIRAGE	62
STONEWASHED TRUTH	63
(cont) STONEWASHED TRUTH	64
PREDESTINY	66
THE RIFT	68
SACRED CRANNIES	70
SUNSET DRIVES	72
AMBIENT MIST	74
SIPPIN' SOUND BITES	77
AFRICAN MOONLIGHT	78

BURNING RUBBER ON THE STONES	80
HAVENS	82
THE WAY GOD SPEAKS	83
HOW WE PAINT THE PHOTOS YELLOW	84
A COWBOY SONG AND AN ENDLESS TOAST	85
A COUNTRY NIGHT	87
EYES FULL OF COBBLESTONE	89
JESTER	90
ORIGINS	91
INDIGO ANGEL	92
(cont) INDIGO ANGEL	94
SUNDAY DRIVES	95
A GOLDEN VESSEL	97
THE SACRED GONG SHOW	98
WIND	100
INTANGIBLE TOUCH	101
LETTING IT BE	103
A JADE SHADOW	104
ABOUT THE AUTHOR	105

DEDICATION

This book is dedicated to Stephen, Mom, Mom and Dad...and my hope is that it touches readers with as much spirit as my family has faith in these deep poems. without them my poetry would still be scattered on hard drives in deep sleeps...I also want to dedicate the collection of poems to my spiritual Mother, Father, Teacher, and Friend ...God. Although writing poetry evolved from personal pain, living poetry—even if only in moments—came from the stillness, the beauty, and a love of God. These poems come from all places between the heights of realization and understanding, and low grips of human— ness when life seemed out of control, spilling me over the edges. The poems are the steps between the stars and steel fingers, a journey many of us take on our quest for meaning and magic.

GREENLIGHT DARES

The old world

creeps in

through the mouse hole,

and you can still smell yesterday… the first day love hurt, the

second day you learned to speak

while standing at a distance from yourself.

Still. outside the wind stirs,

and something larger than your

sense of duty calls you,

the sound of the river

like a shy African drum,

the fireflies…orderly as stars

spinning in orbits

over the grass and beneath the moon.

Something wild calls you

because your belly

is stuck on yesterday

and you need something different to eat.

something like a backwards crawl

to California, a gourmet moon,

or a greenlight dare.

TWO SISTERS AND A SHORE

We picnicked on the grass,

tossed a soggy football,

and made warrior dives into an icy pool.

That's what the night was made of....

...of conversations

about the old days,

ones we wished we could go back to

for electricity.

We planted our toes along seawalls

and left our fears as small

as ants in the grass.

Child giants, we serenaded the moon,

with "Vincent" and "The Tin Soldier."

We were loose in the air,

the sea had stolen our skins,

and all that was left was

the part of ourselves

that howl and sing and make nonsense,

that part age packs away

like someone who folds underwear in triangles

and piles them in pancakes in the drawer.

(cont) Two Sisters

We planted our toes along seawalls

and giggled deeply,

defiant in an innocent way,

like children who never learned the rules,

who never broke their spirits to belong.

There were no sugared words, no combed hairs,

no pauses before speaking.

That is what the night was made of.

…of green, of saltwater breath,

and jailbird laughter.

It was made of sand with open eyes

and the freedom of a child

that comes before the lies

and not after.

Solitude is only bearable with God.

ANDRE GIDE

GOD'S WISH

You just want us to shine,

to come out of tunnels,

into the sound of maracas,

into the green of trees

into smiles as soft as old cotton T-shirts.

And you don't need a thing.

You don't crave a crumb.

Your love is to draw us

out of small boxes and sleepover nightmares,

into dreams and open meadows

with every drip of you

sweetening the grass.

You sew the seeds of spring

and give us the chance to live,

to spill rainbows

and spend idle days

making lightning and laughter

from the air.

And you tell us the truth,

again and again

with patience as solid as stone,

"Remember me, sweet child.

Let go and remember me."

LAKEWATER OF STARS

Let the letters of your name crumble

and set your suit by the door.

Cast your eyes far enough

into the lake water of stars

to see that what seems normal is

actually strange, things like

five o' clock traffic, rituals of feeding the dog,

dropping the children off at the bus stop,

walking in and out of work

in and out of work

and in and out of home.

Cast your eyes far enough into

the lake water of stars

to see how revolving doors

can hypnotize the soul,

how they put you to sleep

in the ticks of a clock.

A thousand thoughts go by

and cities pass briskly

like children pressing out of school doors,

and all the while.

you forget that you are steering,

that your feet are the wheels

and your eyes the headlights staring

down a lifetime of highways.

(cont) LAKEWATER OF STARS

You pass in and out of rooms

filled with holiday ripples,

into corners stuffed with secrets,

and onto landing pads made

of gold and gravel.

But cast your eyes far enough

into the lake water of stars

to see that truth

is not in your shoes of grass

or the letters of your name

 but in the quiet free beauty, that

in and out of revolving doors,

remains the same.

THE ODD STREAM

Silly sojourns take you

Into freckle-faced places,

places like people you never thought

you would talk to.

but then you hear their words,

chimes that are two steps from your front door.

not as far as you thought.

And the people, and the people

still bow their heads to pray.

Even in Central Park,

they collect crumbs like rosary beads.

And the ducks, and the ducks

follow them.

How can you expect them not to?

We push. They push. We push.

and nature is a never ending mirror

we knock our heads on.

Has anyone brought the dolls

down from the garret?

Just wanted to say that word,

put it on like red lipstick,

wear it like a cosmetic veneer.

(cont) THE ODD STREAM

Where are the people going?

The ducks went the other way

and we are not in sync

and the poor moon is like a director

with a muffled voice.

Who can hear him saying step left

over the wind?

Just eat the berries. They're good for you.

Roll them like electricity in your belly

and you will shine.

You will make the rooftops shy

and the sky will blush

and you will dance without make-up

in a midnight rush.

NEW SKIN

I watched the children playing.
as fresh as newly lit firecrackers,
swimming in the cool water for hours,
making fish turns and building homes
between the bubbles.

And the adults.
They took a dip in too
but it was an inch by inch thing.
No screams. No splashes.

The children made a life inside the water
and everything became taffy for them.
a loosened leaf, a flying Elmo doll,
a pipeline fantasy on a still boogie board.

They were living from the inside out
and that's what made them
so interesting to watch.

Who wouldn't like to see
a thought swim inch by inch
to the lips, or the embryo
of a smile grow?

(cont) NEW SKIN

And the adults.

They took a dip in too,

but it was an inch by inch thing.

No screams. No splashes.

The children bared their souls.

showed their ankles,

and urged me, without speaking,

to offer more

than epidermal flashes.

INDIAN DYES

We just waded there in Lake Jenny Jewel,

making circles with our toes in the algae,

looking into the corners we had been since childhood.

Even now, we still float on our backs

and roll our bellies in the sun,

prattling back and forth.

We spoke about how our houses

had been each other's havens,

about the old wooden playhouse

and our neighborhood outing

in ten year old skins

wrapped in pantyhose and balloons.

We volleyed there on the water

between spaces of laughter

like wells being sprung

and spaces of emptiness

where too many steps

had been taken from our roots.

I realized on that day

what a blessing Karlye

had been to my childhood,

how she had been like sparklers

or a bag of giggles in a blank wood room.

(cont) INDIAN DYES

And we had grown differently,

just like the cypress trees on the bank,

but life is magical that way,

how it never tells us who we will be.

It just lets us float in and out with

faces that get both fuller and emptier

each time we see each other.

Our souls collide with so many in this world,

and each person shares with us a color.

Most of the hues vanish and fade,

but there are some

who are like Indian dyes on fine silk,

and like Karlye, again and again

come into and but never out of our hearts.

You have to leave room in life to dream.

BUFFY SAINTE-MARIE

FREEDOM SONG

You have the right to say anything,

to bring nonsense into the light,

to shake it like cobwebs over fine silver

or wear it like biker boots at a debutante ball.

You have the right to say anything,

and as long as you don't leave scars,

you have the right to wear white

when the grass says blue.

There are days when solitude is a heady wine that intoxicates you with freedom, others when it is a bitter tonic, and still others when it is a poison that makes you beat your head against the wall.

COLLETTE

A SONG TO THE DIVINE

He left his shoes

unlaced on the bank

and with bare feet,

stumbled onto the tight wood dock.

His eyes were like golf balls

wrapped in teary velvet skin,

and he howled to the river,

"Let me in! Let me in!"

.into the water

where there are tears enough,

nothing more to lose.

Let me touch the bottom where

the sand is easy to fall on,

And show me some beginning

or some end because I'm tired

of going around, around,

of talking about weather,

and putting on brakes

before I look in.

Most of all

I'm tired of not knowing

why I'd rather stand still

or walk in circles

when You have drawn a window in my eye

and shown me precisely what to do.

We are beings in a school for gods in which we learn in slow motion the consequences of thought.

WM. BRUGH JOY

THE WARM ETERNITY

The best place to dream

is where the grass holds your footprint

and waits for you to come back again

You find solitude in only what you take to it.

JUAN RAMON JIMENEZ

IF NOT TODAY

I'll meet You on the corner
where newspapers sleep on laps
and turn to alphabets in the wind.

I'll meet You on the mountain
where the lucid footsteps go
and ten feet above the ground
where my bones hang low.

And I'll see you somewhere,
somewhere I have yet to see,
where my eyes look like You
and I feel all of me.

I'll meet You somewhere,
somewhere I have yet to go,
where the years turn to ashes
nd our love goes slow.

The mind is like a boomerang... the farther you cast it, the richer its return.

ANNIE LONDON PITTS

ZERO

Have you ever watched

fish weeds on the wall

or sipped cold tea

to the backdrop of street-yard voices?

Have you ever reeled yourself

again and again from sound,

back to the starting line,

to the dock before the fish bit,

to the second before you moved,

to the zero before you ever thought

of ten and twenty?

To live several lives, you have to die several deaths.

FRANCOISE GIROUD

UNARMED WHISPERS

She left the silver paint

from her slipper

in the sidewalk grass, and

it faded after two nights.

Dad stayed inside

chipping at memories

caked like yellow on the walls,

knocking old echoes

out of a childlike silence

that feared intrusion.

He hid tears

like stolen pennies,

wiped up emotions

and brought home

pockets full of green

o four children

who tiptoed behind him.

We stole the antique stories

from the air,

warmed ourselves

in the residual fragrance

of our mother,

and searched for a place to feel,

a place to cry a tear

with no skin and

speak in unarmed whispers

in search of healing.

There are only two or three human stories, and they go on repeating themselves as fiercely as if they'd never happened before.

WILLA CATHER

LOSING NAME

Today, my name is "Bebe."

Yesterday it was "Ethiopian Bone Child."

and tomorrow it will be

"Limb-less on the North Star".

a soul who, like every other human being,

will have to let go,

to learn to sip truth,

and walk in waking eyelids,

and shed the weight to see.

To have one's individuality completely ignored is like being pushed quite out of life. Like being blown out as one blows out a light.

EVELYN SCOTT

HOME

Home is not four walls
stained with the frequency
of hopes,
but a space inside.
a comfort that feels like
being lulled into a good night's sleep,
a gentle breeze with nothing behind it
except idle time waiting
to be filled with spontaneity.

Home is a silent, simple space.
It's allowing yourself to be
both broken and mended.
It's a street you can walk down barefoot
or a wave of love you can get lost in
without having to think
about whether
you are in the Pacific or the Atlantic.

Home is a stranger
you can enter without speaking.
a sacred space you travel far to touch
though have never left.
But, it's the memory of home

that puts the muscle in your steps

when you would rather stick your soul in a corner and turn to wood.

Home is who you are,

and the rest is where you go before you

realize how much you need to get back.

CAUTION

Stick to outlined streets

trimmed with precision

and you're bound

to roll on an empty bell

towards a dissolving sun,

eclipsed by the pain

of a packaged dream.

THE QUEEN

The golden apple

stands on treetops,

bold enough

to touch the sky,

to roll on shadows and

challenge them to bend.

Even her stem is noble,

the way it points

towards the heavens and

stares into the Milky Way

as if she is chaste

of the creature comforts,

the skin of leaves,

the firelight of earth.

There's something grand about open windows that let poetry ooze inside like rich, thick cream from the delivery wagon to nourish our souls.

ANNIE LONDON PITTS

WINDOWSILLS

There must be

a thousand shades

rom this windowsill

of silence,

this place where

all of a sudden,

the eye is loosened

from its socket like a coin.

Now I see the aqua lips of water,

the bluebird skimming rooftops

like a daydream.

Now the world is still.

The green leaves of trees

are praying.

And a white angel's voice

peers into our hearts,

her whispers

wind on waking embers.

There must be

a thousand shades

from this windowsill

of silence,

this place where

all of a sudden,

the heart is loose.

the world is still.

and the eye

begins to see.

We shall not cease from exploration. And the end of all our exploring will be to arrive where we started and know that place for the first time.

T.S. ELIOT

WIND AND ROOTS

Today, I will be a butterfly

who has learned to speak

of womb-cycles and wings.

I will loosen myself in eternity

and tiptoe out of these human scraps

that have held me from truth

as if it were a storm

I was unable to enter.

Today, I will find myself in You,

sweetened, softened, craving spiritual love

deeper than

bon-bons and lily buds.

Today, I will be

both wind and roots.

I will sift the sky,

yet tie myself

to Your silence

like dogwood veins

set on loving the soil.

*When you have shut your doors and darkened your room,
remember never to say that you are alone; for you are not
alone, but God is within and your genius is within.*

EPICTETUS

QUIET LIGHTNING

It only takes one soul

on fire with the flame of truth

to make you into something

you thought you weren't,

something new

like a painting on the wall

or gossamer in a midnight breeze.

It only takes one soul

on fire with the truth

to turn the room upside down

and shake the thick line loose.

To the poet, to the philosopher, to the saint, all things are friendly and sacred, all events profitable, all days holy, all men divine.

EMERSON

ONE INSOMNIAC DREAM

A silent snow,

a subtle smile,

one insomniac dream in

a white haze

that holds me in your eyes.

You watch me

while I sleep, Lord,

leave Your word

on my lips ...

an alphabetic touch

that sways.

then whispers and grows distant,

lost.until I return

inside a silent snow,

a subtle smile,

and one insomniac dream

ON SOLID SKY

I am free.

I have left my eyes

on the shore

and am learning to dance

with no hands,

to tiptoe across the stars

like crumbs leading me home.

And in this deep indigo,

I am rolled up,

distant from your opinion.

I can't hear you anymore,

but now that I can see,

I understand you,

so I've left a space

for you to join me.

SUMMER MOON

Summer moon.

We held you in our palms,

and carried you

onto skins of soil and lake water.

We sent you rolling

through ballerina oaks.

Summer moon.

We stole you

to see what the sky

looked like without you,

to see the souls

all lit up like candles,

swaying in the rain

and drinking stardust,

thinking of home.

because the sky

was too dark

without the sound of your name.

Strange we never prize the music 'til the sweet-voiced bird has flown.

MAY RILEY SMITH

ETERNITY

She made a circle in the glass,

framed in faded wood

and cracks and with her eyes,

tiptoed past fences and neighbors,

broke open a pocket of time,

turned it inside out

and spilled the contents,

the history of her soul.

illogical streams of weathered faces,

Irish landscapes,

baked linen in the breeze,

slow motion laughter,

love like a Carolina porch swing,

and moments, moments like knots

where what once was open

had learned to hide.

They were stories she had always felt

like the way you sense the coming of the rain,

but on that day

the stream was clear,

and she could finally see enough prose

to touch eternity

and feel it breathe.

YOU ARE

I am the eye

that has been spinning

inside this earth,

the one who dreams

and finds solace

in the memory of You.

I curl into You like silk

and pose in serenity.

I thirst for a day of truth,

a place where

the sun and the moon

exchange the spotlight,

and the rains fall between them

like the silence

between two beats.

(cont) YOU ARE

I am the one

who loses the nectar of time,

each moment a chance

to oppose the dark

and reveal beauty

escapes.

I am the one

who longs for communion,

for love with no broken spaces,

no seat for fear to abide.

I break the tips of pain inside

and bend them into circles

that cushion me,

and softer now.

I grow close to You.

I am the one who is healing.

WIGGLER'S FARMER'S MARKET

I was a quarter of an inch deep in mud,
pulling myself deeper into the market.
My eyes strolled lash by lash
and I breathed the new world in.

I guess I had grown too used to cement walls
cooled with man-made breath
because this was something like lightning,
and it shook me the way a naked moonlight does
out of "nine to five."

There was a myriad of flowers.
hyacinth, Gerber daisies, violets, and mums.
Each one sipped in the warm gray day
and drank the rain like an afternoon tea.

You could smell the cedar stands.
You could hear them moan and see them bend
like old men's bones about to give in
but going on anyway to tell the tales
of the way life used to be
when everything was simple.

I wasn't sure if anything human lived there,
but I pressed the service button anyway,

not sure if something was going to grow from the mist. Instead,
I heard a foghorn like a red carpet
rolling out the next scene.

(cont) WIGGLER'S FARMERS MARKET

There she was.an antique piece of country,

a thousand miles from my world,

but she stepped into me

because my eyes were wide enough

to let her in.

She was wearing mud the way an apple wears caramel,

and was uncombed and perfumed in earth and fish.

The shack behind her was on crutches,

and the door was halfway open

as if there were secrets left to keep the story stirring.

I had to come back to myself.

I did what I came to do.

I bought the worms and gave her a $1.50.

I tried to build a bridge and tell her what they were for, but she smiled and seemed un-phased.

Our bodies were three feet apart,

but there were a thousand miles between us,

and that's what made it beautiful,

like drinking in a new country

or smelling for the first time.

I was a quarter of an inch deep in mud.

I was lost in her rhythm and the rhyme.

The nurse of full-grown souls is solitude.

JAMES RUSSELL LOWELL

CHILI SAUCE

Sesame oil, garbanzo beans,

chili sauce and dry spaghetti

on white rubber racks.

Moonlight sweeps over them

the way a child's fingers

tuck toys beneath the bed.

I would like to think of You, God,

but sometimes,

I think of chili sauce instead.

COMMUNION

I saw you, oak tree,

early in the morning,

holding the stars

as if to promise the

a position near the sun.

At the same time, you bent your limbs to the soil, whispering some secret in your veins.

What I heard was the tale of a child passing from a womb into a fantasy of freedom only to find his tears on your hips, growing years on your rings.

I heard you whisper of a young girl with a dream hot inside of her palms, dancing on flames towards an enchanted destiny and of lost love resting its eyes on home.

(cont) COMMUNION

You know, Oak Tree,

your whisper sounds like silence

to the world,

but voices unheard

form deep communions.

After all, the soil

keeps twisting doorknobs to let you in,

and the pillow for the sky

is your promise

to keep her free and high.

MIRAGE

If there's anything worth learning,

it's that desire

can often lead you

into the pale smoke of a mirage.

Unless there are firecrackers

in your soul,

sure of direction,

it can be dangerous to want.

Wanting feels like elastic bands

popping back and forth

over your peace of mind.

And you may think

you want a skyscraper

or a fingerprint sacred enough

to hold gazes like pennies

in a piggy bank,

but that is the small part of you,

the part that wants

to come in like trumpets

because it's not sure if anyone is listening.

(cont) MIRAGE

If there is anything worth learning,

it is to crave only the things

that no one can take away,

like the knowledge of deep love

or the ability to stand on one toe

in beauty and strength without being shaken.

If there is anything worth craving,

it is the desire

to make your eyes into beacons

and your soul sweet enough

to work like milk

on the empty belly of the world.

STONEWASHED TRUTH

Stone crisp white ceilings

wear the shadows

of memory.

Glass panes wash

this hurried world

to my fingers

and a slow breeze

lulls me into mediocrity.

The temperatures are sleepy

and I can barely feel You

pointing to what is real.

I spent too many seconds

in voices that framed life

in small circles,

that told me love

was a consolation,

a warm body

to ward off the honesty of silence.

(cont) STONEWASHED TRUTH

I just want to hear you.

I wish you would speak up.

shake the curtains,

shrink the shadows.

or something.

But, I know.

I should know by now

how you work,

how you come in and out

between silence and static.

So, I'll console myself with that.

I'll stop wrestling

and hope for something magic,

something like the sound

of the moon rubbing at the day

or the gift to be sensitive,

even in sleep, to the silence you speak.

Nothing is more revealing than movement.

MARTHA GRAHAM

PREDESTINY

Cold pickles and a half eaten apple

on the edge of a vine clothed fence.

They bend toward the sun

because they're as tired as we are.

And the doves, they sing in flocks above,

loosening themselves like clean sheets

drying in the wind.

Again and again.

what feels new is forgotten choreography.

Open screens and rocking chairs

wild as your passions.

back and forth…back and forth.

Sometimes I go about pitying myself, and all the time I'm being carried on great wings across the sky.

CHIPPEWA INDIAN PROVERB

THE RIFT

Today, I am the word

on the edge of your lip,

afraid to speak.

electric barbwire.

swaddled dream.

Today, you are the line

on the next page.

a fetal love

and a thousand hands

on the other side

of this country.

I think somehow we learn who we really are and then live with that decision.

ELEANOR ROOSEVELT

SACRED CRANNIES

Picket fences scrub the grass

the way a mystic does its own soul

in hopes of coming clean.

Picket fences listen to crickets sleep

and daisies bend

and the mystic listens

to the sound of God on the wind,

the quietest whisper to wash them to the sea.

The picket fence may not be for you,

but for the one who is comfortable

in human skin,

the picket fence

is the sound of God on the wind.

Between whom there is hearty truth, there is love.

HENRY DAVID THOREAU

SUNSET DRIVES

The kitchen debate,

a sister spat

and scattered boxes from the move.

one day left behind.

Peeled by the wind,

I drove and drove to You

to be free again.

Drove into freshly painted skies

and over speed limits,

up with seagulls

and onto daylight's dying embers.

We go so slowly into You,

like an old woman's steps,

slow, so we can see.

slow, so we can be sure

slow, so we can feel ourselves

peeled by the wind.

We drive and drive to You to be free again.

If you're not feeling good about you, what you're wearing outside doesn't mean a thing.

LEONTYNE PRICE

AMBIENT MIST

Ambient mist

all gray over the earth,

You muffle our voices

to urge us to scream.

Even the simplest tree frog

hunts for higher ground

all because of your skin

over us.

But when you clear,

ray by ray,

the sunlight will shine in

like a mother seeking the source

of her child's tears.

Then we will all be green

and pink and orange and yellow,

as wild as a peacock's feathers,

back home to color

and the lambent glow of truth.

Ambient mist.
You may hide the height of the grass
and swallow the horizon,

but the Sun will seek you out

and send you

drop by drop

into the sky,

packed like a winter sweater

at the end of spring.

The real in us is silent; the acquired is talkative.

KAHLIL GIBRAN

SIPPIN' SOUND BITES

Today was about placing electric moons on dried
leaves,
Of finding new ways to see,
New ways to listen so that
Instead of residual gab
There's a pocket full of sound bites:

"I was sad to see fairyland go."
"Someone still needs to find the electric moon."
"The blueberry cake has no eggs."
"Remembrance is the same thing as company,"
God says.

Sounds strewn together like silk patches,
Some new way to listen,
Some new way to lick salts from the sea,
And burn rubber on hard ice
To let the water out to speak.

AFRICAN MOONLIGHT

The sea crests were salty and cool,

clinging to our ankles

like children who loved us,

and the moon,

it hung over the sand and the souls,

an ice cube cooling our flushed faces.

We danced to the beat of the drums,

in the sea.on the sand,

in spaces each beat

cleared from the sky.

We chipped at human density

and slow heartbeats.

We came with the music

into clear oxygen.

far from the world

and close to home.

Energy is the power that drives every human being. It is not lost by exertion but maintained by it.

GERMAINE GREER

BURNING RUBBER ON THE STONES

So the river is frozen.

Nothing moves you.

Stories are lazy teens

growing roots to sheets and tubes.

Music is something someone else plays

and prayers hang out

in your pockets

like phone numbers lost on scraps.

You stand still and act like stone,

stone because you're so stuck

on being stuck that nothing gets in.

And what's stuck grows cold.

What's cold freezes.

Still, you can melt water

with the heat of resolve

and break the ice

by burning rubber on the stones.

Where love reigns the impossible may be attained.

INDIAN PROVERB

HAVENS

Of all the havens

that I've crawled into,

the warm arms

that turned to ice,

the spoonful of applesauce,

the quiet corners where

the branches of oaks

pretended to be blankets.

Of all the havens

that I've crawled into,

your heart is the only place

that has healed me, that has taken me

far enough from these walls

to become what I haven't been for years.

a child, a tender light.

soft because there's nothing to fear,

warm because the distance

was made of earth,

and alive because I need

nothing more than you

to feel like living.

THE WAY GOD SPEAKS

I hear church bells on Austrian hills

and quiet chimes dangling

from a clay ceiling in Peru.

I hear the brush of palms

on cool caves and

tears drifting as high as the stars.

I hear footsteps soft in the grass,

hiding and searching. and

Spanish music dripping on alleys.

I hear the life in slow motion.

soft the way God whispers

when you scream.

HOW WE PAINT THE PHOTOS YELLOW

The canaries perch

on triangle points

of the fence.

They sing Chinese to me but maybe

English to the grass.

We watch ants build in the garden

and drink watermelon juice.

We string the beans

and listen to

the absence of rock and roll

the hum of neighbors

like wind on cornstalks.

We learn to breathe,

to smell the earth,

ripe tomatoes and

grape juices leaking on leaves,

dogwoods and sweet grass.

This is how we rub holes in garden sheds,

how we paint the photos yellow,

This is simple beauty,

the open eye simmering

the juice of memory.

A COWBOY SONG AND AN ENDLESS TOAST

He taught me how to dangle

a cigarette on my lip, how

to wear a cowboy hat

and hang out of a truck at 16.

But it wasn't smoking he was teaching.

it was the wildness,

the lively spirit that drinks the moon

before it sleeps, and names

the color of every fish

before the sun sets.

He can enter a broken

engine or human part

and tic and turn

until it's right side up with a beating heart.

His hands are his gold and

he'll tell you every tale of history told.

Then he'll sit there with

A quivering lip and a tear in his eye

And tell you all about his tough heart with a soft sigh.

He's made of laughter.

He's made of brawn,

Of an open eye

And an eager dawn.

But, most of all

I love in him most.

that cowboy song

And his endless toast.

A COUNTRY NIGHT

It's midnight.

the sun has dripped in streaks.

leaving a puddle to remember

June 6th by.

The wooden wheelbarrow

is full of sweet hay.

wafting outside the cracked wall

where candlelight seeps out

to toast the black night.

Corn stalks whisper

and woo the stars

and country folk

with easy dreams

sleep with tight muscles

and pray on loose seams.

Character builds slowly, but it can be torn down with incredible swiftness.

FAITH BALDWIN

EYES FULL OF COBBLESTONE

In the cobblestone streets,

Nickels scatter like small moons.

Screams come out but sound like whispers.

Insanity is a silent thing.

Tucked in the quiver of a smile.

The sun settles on windowsills and

People grab it with nets of palms.

They wear dark circles beneath their eyes

And drink gossip like whiskey.

Spiders are feasts and

Snakes are kings

In the cobblestone streets

Where people see nothing but things.

JESTER

The jester has a touch of magic.

He lives from a space untaught

That unravels without intention

And shakes people wildly

Giggling over the stars.

He can make a queen's China lips crack

And split a flame into dazzling scarves.

He can make a necklace of the moon

And make the winds swoon.

A sublime fingerprint. he never mimics

Except in jest. the jester heals the world

through laughter

And puts our notions to the test.

A sacred clown so nice to have around

When drama wears lead shoes

And our footsteps sing the blues.

ORIGINS

Yellowed rose is the shade of

Lantana in twilight.

It's the hue you see

Through blue eyes

When they've touched the light,

When they've become

Windows to let you into

A world as warm as a grandmother's lap,

As beautiful as a sunset. It's the

Shade of blushed grapefruit, and

The inside skin of a hybrid rose.

I place it in an envelope and

Send it to you, and yellowed rose

Becomes a new definition.

A Webster hue.

INDIGO ANGEL

The night had bled completely

into the day,

the deep indigo drawn over the sea.

She stalked the sands

and though the souls were

sleeping,

their hearts followed her

like a quiet misunderstood longing.

Pieces,

deep and still beautiful,

wandered with her,

out of their boxes,

into a world

that hadn't found its periphery.

She was a strange angel

with Indian wings in violet blazes,

a Guatemalan canteen to her side,

half-filled with water,

a band of pink flowers

in her hair

and bare thin limbs

that stretched upwards

with an arrowless bow,

gentle, yet full of adventure

as if to galvanize

the stars.

(cont) INDIGO ANGEL

In her face

was a soft pink fire of wonder

trimmed with a cool quiet mystery.

She lured the world into her gaze

and allowed them to

get lost in truth again.

And for an evening,

they waded in forgotten beauty,

tucked deeply inside of her

like secrets

she promised to keep.

SUNDAY DRIVES

The white paper trees

stood there like soldiers

against the routine

I came from.

Sunlight fell through branches,

wooden and webbed.

I almost forgot what poetry

was until I took a wrong turn on a

Sunday drive

and found the world sunny and gentle,

clay in my hands.

An old couple walked hand in

hand. A golfer putted toward the sun

as if to beg it not to set.

Children spun wheels on groomed grass,

and one soft hillside grew

over my memory of streets.

Poetry is made of the same thread as purity,

of freshness.

freshness that makes you look,

slows you down,

makes you feel.

There's not a man alive

that can't take a

wrong turn

on a Sunday drive.

A GOLDEN VESSEL

Sweep the dust

and turn the wooden planks

to gold.

Leave the music

on its invisible wave

and sit down

in the remembrance

of your beginning.

Make yourself golden,

so clean that

the milk of the lioness

fills you, so strong

that your eyes stretch across

the sea and you see what mortals

do not see.

the roots of wind and the

wide-eyed view of time

walking from the beginning to the end.

THE SACRED GONG SHOW

If you look at it the

wrong way,

failure is a saltwater kiss.

It prunes you,

makes you old before your time.

You carry creations and feelings,

fragile blackberries, into minds

armed with forks,

and failure bangs the gong

and makes blackberries bleed

until it's all too much

and you crawl back into the seed.

If you look at it the right way,

failure is sacred.

stillness in an ugly dress. tight.

It puts a shine in your eye

and keeps you walking on platforms

made of sighs.

Failure lets you feel

the steel needle

of the world

and platforms are hurled.
It makes you sit there with your
blurry sight and wrinkled might.
It makes you scream for peace
in the pink twilight.

WIND

It turns still water

into electric ripples,

helmet heads

into beach swept hair.

It bends trees

into exquisite shapes,

and mimics the drama,

pushing against us

to add tenacity,

to help us let go.

Always mysterious. you never know

where it comes from

or where it goes,

but it picks up something more

each place it touches.

Wind is much more than a breeze.

It's history

on the tip of our tongues.

INTANGIBLE TOUCH

I saw them in a pale garden,

a strange frozen couple.

He lingered in circles of his cigarette smoke,

and she looked away in one thoughtless gaze.

They knew no one was home, but

they kept visiting,

coming back again and again

for an intangible touch,

a hope of coming back alive,

even for a moment,

to color the bleakness

that had stained them.

I just stood there and watched them,

their edges chiseled and

cut away from the world behind them,

as if on purpose so they could

stand out and speak.

And I listened. I wanted to

hold them with my eyes

and even stepped out of a moment

and its demands on me

to peel them from the sky

and press them on my mind

as a reminder to melt,

to breathe warmly into the love

that's too cold to travel to the touch.

LETTING IT BE

A silver circle of rain

cups a tear.

It freezes

the edges

so the pain stays there.

I've been wasting my time,

wiping it,

scheming its removal,

when

I should just let it stay

like a scene of time I can pass

and even forget.

Though it may linger deep inside,

behind me,

below me

as the fire

dwells inside the earth,

it is distant enough

not to burn my steps.

A JADE SHADOW

You can see it in the fire

that smokes from the eye,

or a tall walk

that shortens the passersby,

but you can't touch it.

It's a jade shadow

that inhabits the skin and

takes its stabs,

but continues to grow.

It's a fossilized soul,

who, with little space to breathe,

bellies up a frustrated echo

and learns to scream.

And its remedy

is not a quarrel or a restructuring

of systems and traditions,

but a revelation

that the womb of life

is not made of skin, but of a

wandering thought

whose origin and destination

is freedom.

ABOUT THE AUTHOR

Bebe Butler is a graduate of Boston University with a degree in Broadcast Communications. She currently resides in Tampa, Florida, where she is a Creative Arts Specialist with the City of Tampa Performing Arts, providing education to children through legends, myths, storytelling and puppetry. She practices Raja Yoga and is deeply involved with the Brahma Kunari Yoga Center in Tampa.

www.ingramcontent.com/pod-product-compliance
Lightning Source LLC
LaVergne TN
LVHW040155080526
838202LV00042B/3175